sun

mars

neptune

moon

earth

uranus

In Our Solar System

A Counting Poem About Outer Space

Jenny Sundstedt

ILLUSTRATIONS BY
Susanna Covelli

FAMILIUS

Published by Familius LLC, www.familius.com
PO Box 1130, Sanger, CA 93657

Familius books are available at special discounts for bulk purchases, whether for sales promotions or for family or corporate use. For more information, contact Familius Sales at orders@familius.com.

Library of Congress Control Number: 2024947918

Print ISBN 9781641708869
Ebook ISBN 9798893965032

Printed in China
Edited by Abigail W. Tree and Paige Adams
Cover and book design by Brooke Jorden

10 9 8 7 6 5 4 3 2 1

First Edition

For Nathan and David, my moon and sun.
You make this world a brighter place.
Love, Mom

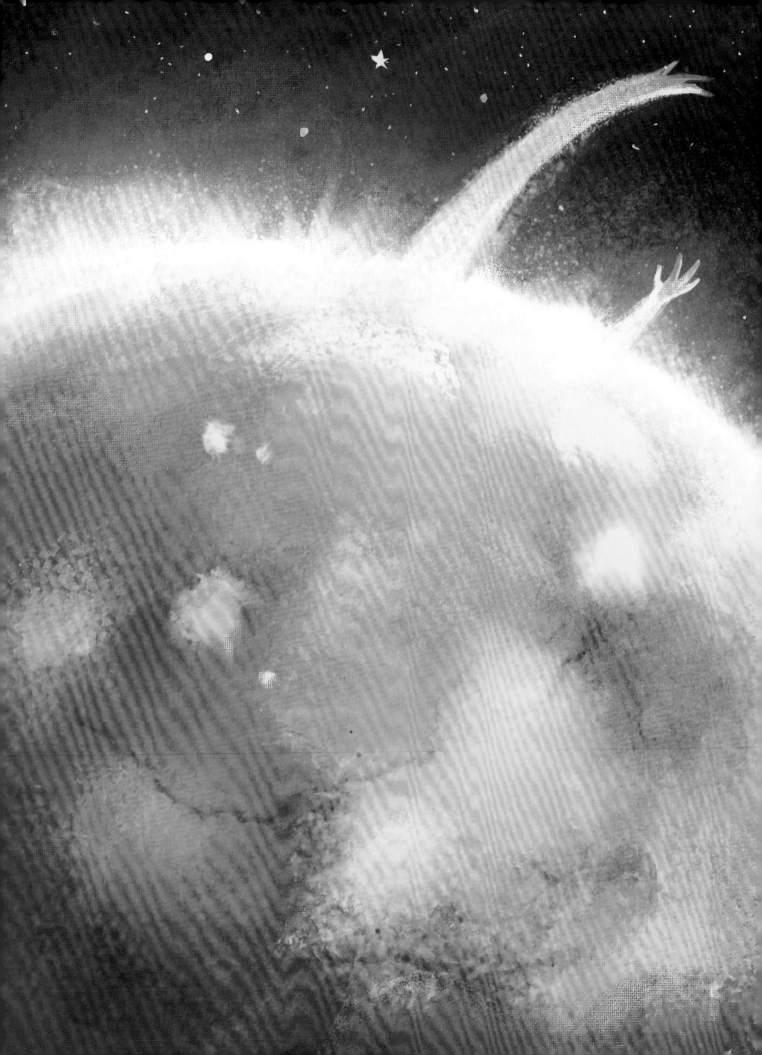

In our solar system,
On the fiery hot sun
Burned a mother solar flare
And her little flare, one.
"Sizzle," said the mother.
"I sizzle," said the one.
So they sizzled and they popped
On the fiery, hot sun.

Our sun is a huge ball of burning gas known as a yellow dwarf star. Around it circle nine-ish planets (more on that later), hundreds of moons, and many more asteroids and comets. A lot happens on and under the sun's surface too. Solar flares burst in sudden explosions of energy. Sunspots—darker, cooler areas—drift along magnetic fields. The inside of the sun roars with noise that can only be heard using special equipment, since sound waves cannot travel through the vacuum of space.

In our solar system,
On a planet speeding through,
Lay a deep father crater
And his little craters, two.
"Yawn," said the father.
"We yawn," said the two.
So they yawned big and wide
On a planet speeding through.

Because Mercury zips around the sun in only
88 days, the Romans named it after the god
of messages, who had wings on his feet. But
even though it orbits quickly, it spins much
slower. That means a single day on Mercury
lasts for about two years there (equal to 176
days on Earth). The planet's rocky surface is
covered with craters named after famous and
often familiar people from all over the world,
including Maya Angelou, William Shakespeare,
Madeleine L'Engle, and Dr. Seuss.

In our solar system,
On a planet hard to see,
Rose a father volcano
And his little cones, three.
"Flow," said the father.
"We flow," said the three.
So they flowed with hot lava
On a planet hard to see.

Although Venus is a planet, it is also called the Morning and Evening Star, since it rises in the night sky at sunset and sets at sunrise. It appears very bright because sunlight shines off its thick layer of clouds (which are full of sulfuric acid). The clouds hold in so much heat that Venus gets the prize for the hottest planet in the solar system, with a temperature around 900 degrees Fahrenheit. The planet's surface is impossible to see from Earth, even with a telescope, but spacecraft that landed there found more volcanoes—including shields, cones, and pancake domes—than anywhere else in the solar system.

In our solar system,
On a night by the shore,
Stood a mother sky-gazer
And her little gazers, four.
"Look," said the mother.
"We look," said the four.
So they looked up in wonder
On a night by the shore.

The name Earth comes from old English and German words that mean "the ground," but almost three-fourths of Earth's surface is covered by water. This home of ours is different from every other planet we know. Like a perfect recipe, it has just the right ingredients—including sunlight, oxygen, and water—to support all kinds of organisms, from microscopic viruses to enormous blue whales. People have searched the skies for hundreds of years, but no one has found life anywhere else in our solar system. It is important to take very good care of this special place.

In our solar system,
Where we might someday arrive,
Rolled a brave father rover
And his little rovers, five.
"Explore," said the father.
"We explore," said the five.
So they explored all around
Where we might someday arrive.

Mars is millions of miles away from Earth,
but it is still close enough for astronauts
to visit in the future. Until then, rovers will
help us learn more about Earth's neighbor.
So far, six rovers have landed on Mars.
They are named Sojourner, Opportunity,
Spirit, Curiosity, Perseverance (which has
its own little helicopter called Ingenuity),
and Zhurong. The rovers have collected
lots of data, photographs, and even audio
that give us an idea of what the Red Planet
looks and sounds like. For example, the
powdery dust covering Mars is full of iron,
which gives it the famous rusty red color.
Sounds are quieter and travel more slowly
through the thin, cold atmosphere.

In our solar system,
On a planet swirled and mixed,
Spun a big mother storm
And her little storms, six.
"Turn," said the mother.
"We turn," said the six.
So they turned and they twisted
On a planet swirled and mixed.

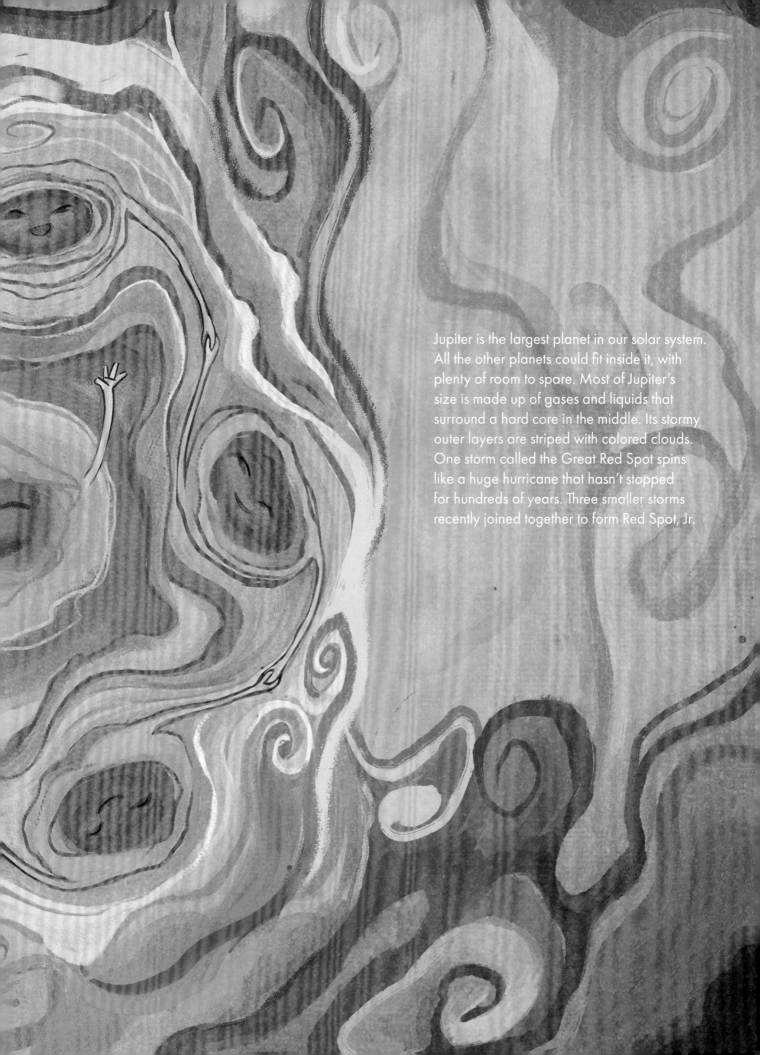

Jupiter is the largest planet in our solar system. All the other planets could fit inside it, with plenty of room to spare. Most of Jupiter's size is made up of gases and liquids that surround a hard core in the middle. Its stormy outer layers are striped with colored clouds. One storm called the Great Red Spot spins like a huge hurricane that hasn't stopped for hundreds of years. Three smaller storms recently joined together to form Red Spot, Jr.

In our solar system,
Far away in the heavens,
Stretched a sparkling father ring
And his little rings, seven.
"Circle," said the father.
"We circle," said the seven.
So they circled loop-de-loops
Far away in the heavens.

Four planets in our solar system have rings around their middles, but
Saturn's are the largest and most recognizable. Chunks of floating
ice reflect the sunlight and make the brilliant rings easy to see with
a telescope. Some of the ice pieces are as small as a speck of dust,
and some are as big as mountains. The rings are held in place by the
gravitational pull of Saturn and four "shepherd" moons, which keep the
particles from escaping into space.

In our solar system,
Where the night was growing late,
Glowed a rocky mother moon
And her little moons, eight.
"Orbit," said the mother.
"We orbit," said the eight.
So they orbited the world
Where the night was growing late.

Scientists pronounce this planet's name "You're-uh-nuss."
It is also called the Tilted Planet because it rotates on its
side. This causes the "days" of total sunlight and "nights"
of total darkness at the poles to last for forty-two years.
Uranus has twenty-seven known moons, many of them
made of ice and rock. One of its moons has the highest
cliff found in the solar system. The view from the top
would look as deep as twelve Grand Canyons.

In our solar system,
Even farther down the line,
Breezed a white mother cloud
And her little clouds, nine.
"Blow," said the mother.
"We blow," said the nine.
So they blew across the skies
Even farther down the line.

From a distance, Neptune's surface looks like a peaceful blue ocean. But it is very stormy, with clouds of frozen methane blown along by wind speeds that exceed 1,000 miles per hour. Though Neptune is known as an ice giant, the planet is very hot under its blanket of clouds. Scientists think the extreme heat and pressure in Neptune's atmosphere can cause rain made of diamonds.

In our solar system,
Near the object at the end,
Streaked a quick father comet
And his little comets, ten.
"Blaze," said the father.
"We blaze," said the ten.
So they blazed shining trails
Near the object at the end.

An American astronomer discovered Pluto in 1930, and an 11-year-old British girl named it. Pluto is so far away that our sun would look like a bright star in the night. Despite this vast distance, comets travel from an area near Pluto called the Kuiper (k-eye-per) Belt all the way to Earth and beyond. In 2006, Pluto's status was changed to a dwarf planet, but even now, not everyone agrees. No matter what it is called, tiny Pluto will always have a special place in far-off space.

At over 4 ½ billion years old, our solar system is positively ancient. Yet each year, scientists learn more new things about it. What will they discover next? Signs of life in the clouds of Venus? Another planet hiding in our solar system? The secrets of lightning on Jupiter? Our sun and the planets that orbit around it hold many exciting mysteries waiting to be solved.